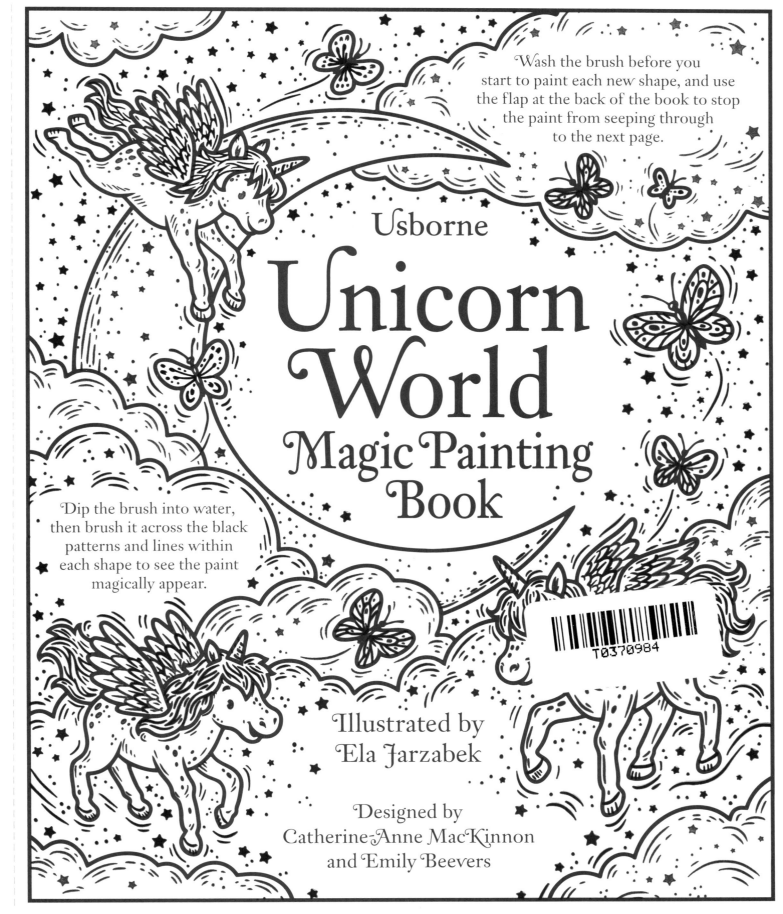

Wash the brush before you start to paint each new shape, and use the flap at the back of the book to stop the paint from seeping through to the next page.

Usborne

Unicorn World
Magic Painting Book

Dip the brush into water, then brush it across the black patterns and lines within each shape to see the paint magically appear.

Illustrated by
Ela Jarzabek

Designed by
Catherine-Anne MacKinnon
and Emily Beevers